# OLIVER
## AT THE
# WINDOW

WRITTEN BY
**Elizabeth Shreeve**

ILLUSTRATED BY
**Candice Hartsough McDonald**

FRONT STREET
*Honesdale, Pennsylvania*

When his parents moved into separate houses,
Oliver started at Redbird School.

There were piles of blocks for building castles,
a puppet-show stage, and more books than
Oliver had ever seen.

Oliver didn't care.
He stood at the window,
holding his lion,
while the other kids played.
He watched the spider weave
secret webs behind the curtain.
He pressed his nose to the glass
and felt the cool air outside.
And he waited for his mom,
or his dad, to pick him up.

Sometimes Oliver went to his dad's house,

sometimes to his mom's. He was never quite sure.

ANIMAL OF THE WEEK:
POLAR BEAR!

If the gate clanged and the door banged,
that was his dad, with a high five and a great big hug.
Oliver's lion got a hug, too.

If the gate squeaked and the door swished open,
that was his mom, with a smile and three kisses
for the top of Oliver's head. Lion got a kiss, too.

All through the fall
as the leaves turned red and gold,
Oliver waited at the window.
He waited a little bit less each day.

"Come." Miss BB smiled. "Let's make some art!"
Oliver painted a picture of his mom's house.

He drew his dad's.
He put his lion in the windows of both.

"Will you be our napkin captain?"
asked Miss BB at lunchtime.

Oliver laid out lots of napkins, lined up in straight rows.
Then he and the lion and all the other kids ate lunch.

"Playtime!" yelled Jack.
Oliver ran outside.

He threw a ball to Miss BB,
pedaled the new bike,
and swung on the big swing.
His lion waved from the steps.

Oliver almost forgot about waiting at the window,
until one morning when the first snowflakes
swirled in the sky.

"Today we have a new friend," said Miss BB.
The new girl stood at the window.
She hugged a fuzzy blanket tight in her arms.
She cried and cried.

Oliver picked up his lion
and went to stand
by the new girl.
He pointed to the spider
behind the curtain.

He blew a puff of steam
on the glass. "Look," he said,
and with his fingertip
he drew two eyes, two ears,
a nose, and some whiskers.

"Is it a dog?" whispered the girl. "Or a cat?"

"It's my lion," Oliver told her. "And I hold him like this."

He showed the girl how his lion was soft, silky,
and just the right size.

Then he rubbed a paw on her face to wipe the tears away.

The girl smiled a tiny smile.

She tickled Oliver's arm with a corner of her
fuzzy blanket. They both laughed.

"Snack time!" called Miss BB.
Oliver's tummy rumbled.

"Let's go," he said to the girl.
"My lion will wait here for us."

For David—*E.S.*
For my family—*C.H.M.*

Text copyright © 2009 by Elizabeth Shreeve
Illustrations copyright © 2009 by Candice Hartsough McDonald
All rights reserved
Printed in China
Designed by Helen Robinson
First edition

Library of Congress Cataloging-in-Publication Data
Shreeve, Elizabeth.
Oliver at the window / Elizabeth Shreeve ;
illustrated by Candice Hartsough McDonald. — 1st ed.
p. cm.
Summary: When Oliver's parents move into separate houses,
he spends a lot of time looking out of windows with his pet lion
as he adjusts to a new preschool and to living in two places.
ISBN 978-1-59078-548-5 (hardcover : alk. paper)
[1. Divorce—Fiction. 2. Moving, Household—Fiction.
3. Schools—Fiction.]
I. McDonald, Candice Hartsough, ill. II. Title.
PZ7.S559148Oli 2009       [E]—dc22
2008022290

FRONT STREET
An Imprint of Boyds Mills Press, Inc.
815 Church Street
Honesdale, Pennsylvania 18431

Little, Brown and Company

Hachette Book Group
1290 Avenue of the Americas, New York, NY 10104
Visit us at lb-kids.com

Little, Brown and Company is a division of Hachette Book Group, Inc.
The Little, Brown name and logo are trademarks of Hachette Book Group, Inc.

The publisher is not responsible for websites (or their content) that are not owned by the publisher.

First Edition: October 2016

Library of Congress Control Number: 2016949440

ISBN 978-0-316-27155-4

10 9 8 7 6 5 4 3 2 1

CW

Printed in the United States of America

# MARVEL
# DOCTOR
# STRANGE

## The Path to Enlightenment

Adapted by Charles Cho
Illustrated by Ron Lim, Andy Smith, and Andy Troy
Based on the Screenplay by Jon Spaihts, Scott Derrickson, C. Robert Cargill
Produced by Kevin Feige
Directed by Scott Derrickson

LITTLE, BROWN AND COMPANY
New York   Boston

Doctor Stephen Strange is not in New York anymore. Here in Kathmandu, the former surgeon walks the streets looking for Kamar-Taj, a sacred place he believes has the power to heal his terribly wounded hands.

Soon, a mysterious man in a cloak approaches Strange and offers to show him the way to Kamar-Taj. They walk silently through a narrow alley and stop in front of a plain, wooden door. "You sure you have the right place?" Strange finally asks.

The arrogant doctor grows uncomfortable as the man in the cloak stares at him.

"I once stood in your place," the man begins. "And I, too, was disrespectful. So might I offer a piece of advice? Forget everything you think you know."

Briefly humbled, Strange does not expect the large courtyard on the other side of the door.

Soon, Strange meets The Ancient One. The mystic informs Strange that his spirit is able to heal his body. "The reality you know is one of many," she continues. "Free your mind..." With a palm strike, The Ancient One pushes Strange's astral form, or spirit, outside his body. "You've entered the Astral Dimension—a place where the soul exists apart from the body."

Strange is barely able to make sense of what's happened when Mordo makes a new gesture with his hands, altering reality yet again. He explains that this Mirror Dimension is used to travel great distances in an instant.

Strange is terrified as Mordo and The Ancient One show him more. "Why...are you doing this?" he asks. "To show you what you *don't* know," the mystic responds.

Just like that, The Ancient One pulls Strange back into the world as he'd known it. He's changed. While he still wants a cure for his hands, now he wants to learn the ways of The Ancient One. He wants to become a sorcerer.

"Kamar-Taj is not an end to itself," Mordo explains, "but a beginning. Bathe. Rest. Meditate, if you can."

Strange is once again a beginner. Practicing the mystic arts, he is frustrated with himself—the others students are far better. The Ancient One tells Strange he must be less proud before he can succeed.

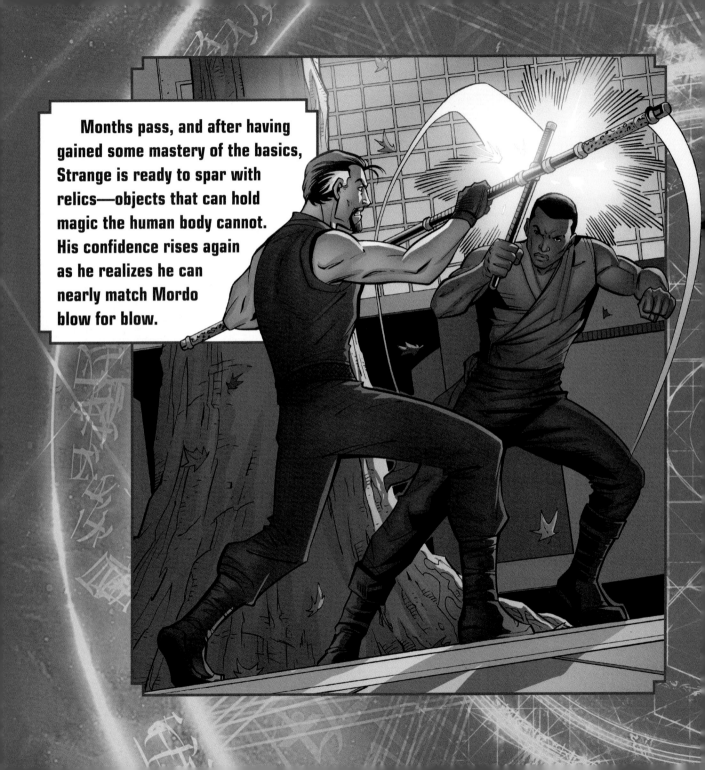

Months pass, and after having gained some mastery of the basics, Strange is ready to spar with relics—objects that can hold magic the human body cannot. His confidence rises again as he realizes he can nearly match Mordo blow for blow.

"Fight like your life depends upon it, because one day, it may," Mordo assures his student. Panting in pain and defeat, Strange realizes he's right. There will be great battles ahead of him.

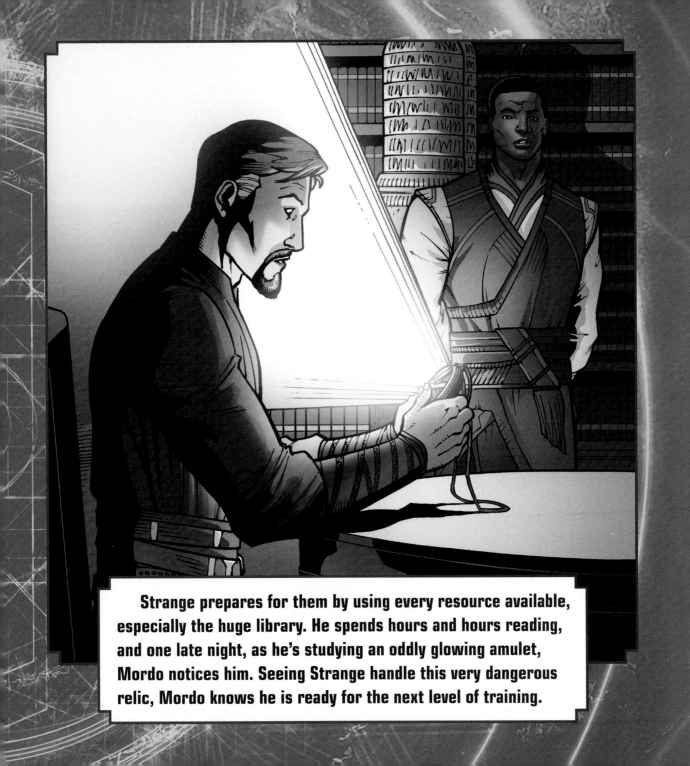

Strange prepares for them by using every resource available, especially the huge library. He spends hours and hours reading, and one late night, as he's studying an oddly glowing amulet, Mordo notices him. Seeing Strange handle this very dangerous relic, Mordo knows he is ready for the next level of training.

Strange then learns that Kamar-Taj is bound to three Sanctum Sanctorums, or secret holy places where the world's sources of power intersect. Just as Strange is adjusting to this new information, an explosion sends him though a gateway back to one of the Sanctums in New York City.

Strange makes his way inside and looks around. It feels like a museum. After a few turns, Strange notices a dark-colored room. Its walls are lined with artifacts. "The Chamber of Relics," Strange states.

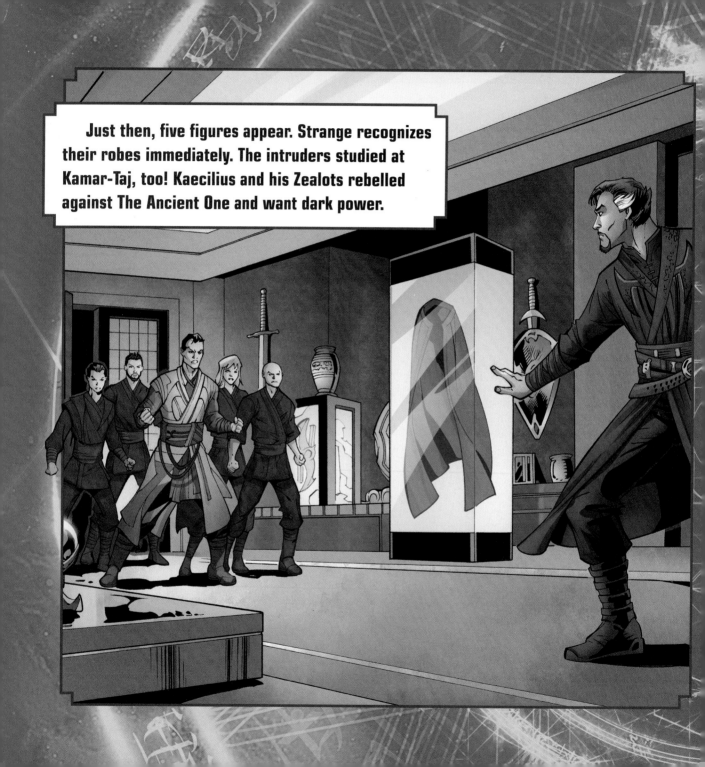

Just then, five figures appear. Strange recognizes their robes immediately. The intruders studied at Kamar-Taj, too! Kaecilius and his Zealots rebelled against The Ancient One and want dark power.

Realizing enemies are in his midst, Strange makes movements with his hands, and a huge crackling flash of energy appears. Strange holds it like a whip and snaps it at the Zealot standing closest to him.

Strange fights the Zealots with everything he has, but he is still learning his craft, and is inexperienced. He puts up as many mandalas as he can, but his powers begin to flicker. Kaecilius launches him into one of the relic cases.

Upon impact, the cloak that was inside the case wraps itself around Strange, protecting him against new attacks. It even makes him float in the air!

He finally has a chance in this fight. Strange is no longer just a wounded surgeon; he is a sorcerer—the Sorcerer Supreme.